P9-DEI-752

AFTER

HAPPILY EVER AFTER

Cinderella and the Mean Queen

First published in the United States in 2009
by Stone Arch Books
151 Good Counsel Drive, P.O. Box 669
Mankato, Minnesota 56002
www.stonearchbooks.com

First published by Orchard Books, a division of Hachette Children's Books.
338 Euston Road, London NW1 3BH, United Kingdom

Library of Congress Cataloging-in-Publication Data
Bradman, Tony.
    Cinderella and the Mean Queen / by Tony Bradman; illustrated by
Sarah Warburton.
    p. cm. — (After Happily Ever After)
    ISBN 978-1-4342-1301-3 (library binding)
    [1. Princesses—Fiction. 2. Fashion—Fiction. 3. Makeover television
programs—Fiction.] I. Warburton, Sarah, ill. II. Title.
PZ7.B7275Ci 2009
[Fic]—dc22   2008031827

Summary: Cinderella's Prince Charming is just perfect, but his mother
is a royal pain. She makes the ugly stepsisters look friendly! With a little
makeover magic, Cinderella is ready to turn the Mean Queen into the
Nice Queen.

Creative Director: Heather Kindseth
Graphic Designer: Emily Harris

            1 2 3 4 5 6 14 13 12 11 10 09

              Printed in the United States of America

AFTER

HAPPILY EVER AFTER

Cinderella and the Mean Queen

by Tony Bradman
illustrated by Sarah Warburton

STONE ARCH BOOKS
www.stonearchbooks.com

So Cinderella and the Prince
lived happily ever after.
And then ...

"Hurry up, Cinderella," said her husband, Prince Charming. "You know Mother hates it when we're late for dinner."

"Coming, sweetheart," Cinderella
murmured. She checked herself one
last time in her full-length mirror.

"What do you think of this dress and these boots?" she asked. "I'm trying out a new style."

"They're fine," the prince said. "Can we go now?"

Cinderella sighed. She loved the prince, and he loved her. She'd thought her troubles were over when they got married.

But it was hard living with Prince Charming's parents in the castle. Everything was so fancy. She missed the little cottage where she had lived with her father.

Sometimes she even missed her
Wicked Stepmother and the Ugly Sisters.
They didn't seem too bad when she
thought about them now.

At least not compared to Prince
Charming's mother, the queen.

"And WHERE have you two been?" the
queen roared as the prince and Cinderella
entered the royal dining room. "Your soup
is getting cold!"

"Sorry, Mother," said the prince.
"You look lovely this evening, my dear,"
said the king, smiling at Cinderella. He
was always very sweet to her.

"You never pay me compliments,"
snapped the queen. The king opened his
mouth to speak, but the queen held up
her spoon and glared.

"Don't bother. I know I look dreadful
these days," the queen went on. "But
I can't spend all day making myself
look pretty. I have more important
things to do!"

Cinderella had a feeling the
queen would like the king to pay her
compliments. She had seen the queen
glancing at herself in mirrors. Then she
would sigh and frown.

The queen was really mean to
Cinderella that evening. Later, Cinderella
sat at her dressing table and cried. The
prince put his arm round her.

"Don't let her upset you, Cinders," he said softly, passing her a royal hanky. "I'm certain Mother likes you. Deep down, anyway."

"No she doesn't," Cinderella wailed.

"She hates me. I've heard her saying I'm useless, and I'm only here because of the Fairy Godmother. Well, I've had enough. I'll prove to her that I'm not just a pretty face."

"Really?" said the prince. "What do you have in mind?"

"I'm going to get a job," said Cinderella. "A good one too."

"Gosh!" said the prince, his eyes wide. "I'm impressed already!"

In the morning, Cinderella looked in the paper. She soon found a job opening. Fairy Tale Fashions, the best clothes store in the forest, was looking for a sales person.

Cinderella had liked clothes and
fashion ever since her own transformation.
She often looked at other people and
thought she might be able to help them.
Maybe give them some advice on how to
improve themselves.

She phoned for an application. She
quickly filled it in, sent it back, and
waited nervously. Her phone rang the
next day.

"Oh hi, yes, this is Cinderella
Charming," she said. "I've got the job?
Wow, fantastic! But wait, aren't you going
to interview me or anything? You're
not, I see. When do I start? Nine o'clock
tomorrow? Okay."

Cinderella was surprised it had been so easy. Surely it should have been harder. After all, she'd never had a real job before. Then she shrugged and started choosing an outfit to wear.

The prince insisted on taking her
to work in the royal coach. But when
they arrived, things weren't quite what
Cinderella had expected.

The royal guards had to hold back a
large crowd. Wild cheering broke out as
Cinderella walked up the red carpet that
led to the store's entrance.

The manager and staff of Fairy Tale
Fashions were there to greet her.

"I don't understand," said Cinderella.
"What are all these people doing here?
I didn't think your big sale started for
another couple of months?"

"They're here to see you, Your Highness," said the manager, curtseying. "What a story! Rags to riches, a grand ball, midnight, the glass slipper—it's all so romantic! Now, there's a TV news crew waiting."

Cinderella's heart sank. She realized Fairy Tale Fashions didn't have a real job for her. They just wanted to use her for publicity. She let the TV crew film her. Then she signed autographs.

Then she got in the royal coach and
went home. She ran up to her room
and burst into tears.

After dinner that evening, the royal
family watched the news. The queen was
even meaner than before.

"What a complete waste of time."
Cinderella heard her say. "She'll never
amount to anything. Plus, she's not
even that pretty."

Cinderella didn't go back to Fairy
Tale Fashions. She phoned them the
next morning and quit.

Cinderella went for a long walk in the royal gardens. She wondered what she should do. Perhaps she could apply for another job. But the same thing would probably happen again. After all, everybody knew her name and her story.

Cinderella was so fed up! She even thought about trying to get in touch with her Fairy Godmother. But she realized that would only prove the queen was right about her.

Whatever she did, she would have to do it without any help. Then Cinderella had an idea.

She spent the rest of that week
planning. She surfed the Forest Web
to see if she had any competition. But
nobody else seemed to be doing what
she had in mind.

A month later she started her business, Cinderella Makeover Limited. She had a big party in the royal ballroom. Lots of people were invited, and the event was covered by Forest TV and all the newspapers.

"They're only interested because she's one of us," the queen said snootily. But Cinderella didn't have time to worry. She was too busy showing everyone what she could do.

A couple of people at the party wanted to be transformed. The results were amazing.

"Wow!" said Little Red Riding Hood's granny when she saw herself.

"I love the way you've done my hair, and these clothes are fantastic! I look at least 20 years younger. I can't thank you enough!"

The queen didn't say a word. She did
seem impressed though.

Soon Cinderella had lots of clients.
She worked her magic on every witch
in the forest, several trolls, and the Bad
Fairy. Not to mention dozens of wicked
stepmothers, including her own, who
turned up one day with the Ugly Sisters.

"If I can help those three out, I can do
anything!" thought Cinderella.

It was a real success. It even led to her getting her own series on Forest TV, *The Cinders Show*.

The Wicked Stepmother and the Ugly Sisters were very grateful. They begged Cinderella to forgive them for being horrible to her in the past. Cinderella did, and from that day on they were great friends.

And not long after that, somebody
else came to see Cinderella in her salon.
It was the queen. She came in, sat
down, and smiled nervously.

"I know I haven't been the best
mother-in-law to you, Cinderella,"
she said. "But I've seen your show on
television, and I just wondered . . ."

Cinderella smiled and got straight to work. She tackled the queen's hair, make-up, and clothes. This time she outdid herself.

That evening, Cinderella and the
queen walked into the royal dining
room together. The prince and the king
were shocked.

"My goodness!" said the king at last, staring at his wife. His eyes were misty with admiration and love. "You look absolutely stunning, dear!"

The queen was delighted, and so was Prince Charming.

"Well done, Cinders!" he said as he kissed her.

And so Cinderella, Prince Charming, his parents, and everyone else in the forest who needed fashion and beauty advice lived **HAPPILY EVER AFTER!**

THE END

ABOUT THE AUTHOR

Tony Bradman writes for children of all ages.
He is particularly well known for his top-selling
Dilly the Dinosaur series. His other titles include
the Happily Ever After series, The Orchard Book
of Heroes and Villains, and The Orchard Book of
Swords, Sorcerers, and Superheroes. Tony lives in
South East London.

ABOUT THE ILLUSTRATOR

Sarah Warburton is a rising star in children's
books. She is the illustrator of the Rumblewick
series, which has been very well received at an
international level. The series spans across both
picture books and fiction. She has also illustrated
nonfiction titles and the Happily Ever After series.
She lives in Bristol, England, with her young baby
and husband.

GLOSSARY

admiration (ad-muh-RAY-shuhn)—a feeling of great approval

competition (kom-puh-TISH-uhn)—a contest of some kind

compliments (KOM-pluh-mentz)—things said to praise someone

curtseying (KURT-see-ing)—a type of bow made by bending the knees and lowering the body slightly

impressed (im-PRESSD)—gained the approval of someone

manager (MAN-a-jur)—a person who is in charge of something

publicity (puh-BLISS-uh-tee)—something used to gain attention from the public

royal (ROI-uhl)—related to a king or queen

transformation (transs-for-MAY-shuhn)—the process of changing into something new

DISCUSSION QUESTIONS

1. Why did Cinderella want to get a job? Why wasn't she happy spending her days in the castle?

2. When her mother-in-law was rude to her, Cinderella never said anything back. Put yourself in her place. How would you respond?

3. How do you think the queen felt about the way she looked before her makeover? Do you think it affected the way she felt about herself and others?

WRITING PROMPTS

1. Cinderella missed parts of her old life. If you were to become a member of a royal family, what would you miss about the life you have now? Make a list of the things you would miss.

2. Fairy Tale Fashions used Cinderella for publicity for the store. She was disappointed, but she still let the television crew film her and signed autographs. Imagine if she had refused instead. Write a few paragraphs about an angry Cinderella at the store opening.

3. Cinderella took her interest in clothes and fashion and turned it into a business. What is one of your interests and how could you turn it into a business? Give your business a name. Write an explanation of what it would sell or what service it would provide.

Before there was **HAPPILY EVER AFTER**,
there was **ONCE UPON A TIME** ...

Read the **ORIGINAL** fairy tales in **NEW** graphic novel retellings.

INTERNET SITES

Do you want to know more about subjects related to this book? Or are you interested in learning about other topics? Then check out FactHound, a fun, easy way to find Internet sites.

Our investigative staff has already sniffed out great sites for you!

Here's how to use FactHound:

1. Visit *www.facthound.com*

2. Select your grade level.

3. To learn more about subjects related to this book, type in the book's ISBN number: **1434213013**.

4. Click the **Fetch It** button.

FactHound will fetch the best Internet sites for you!